The Hippopotamus

River Horse

by Christine and Michel DENIS-HUOT

Charlesbridge

Library of Congress Cataloging-in-Publication Data
Denis-Huot, Christine.
   [l'hippopotame, drôle de sous-marin. English.]
   The hippopotamus, river horse / by Christine and Michel
Denis-Huot.
      p.   cm. – (Animal close-ups)
   ISBN 0-88106-433-5 (softcover)
   1. Hippopotamus–Juvenile literature. [1. Hippopotamus.]
I. Denis-Huot, Michel.   II. Title.   III. Series.
QL737.U57D4513 1994   94-1631
599.73'4–dc20   CIP
                                                                AC

Translated by Siena Cherson and Mark Siegel
Copyright © Éditions Milan 1993.
300 rue Léon-Joulin 31101 Toulouse, France.
Original edition first published by Éditions Milan under the title of *l'hippopotame, drôle de sous-marin*.
French series editor, Valérie Tracqui

The hippo lives in Africa, in rivers, lakes, or anywhere there is fresh water, even if it is muddy or dirty.

The river horse

The river is peaceful on this hot day. Since it hasn't rained in months, the riverbanks are dry and parched. Antelopes cautiously come near the water's edge to drink. They are suspicious and keep an eye on the crocodiles dozing in the sun. An African fish eagle skims the surface of the water looking for fish. The air is hot and the silence is broken only by the screeching of the eagle as it catches a fish in its claws.

In the river, hundreds of hippos look like boulders. Only their eyes, ears, and nostrils stick out of the water so they can see, hear, and breathe while staying cool. They will spend the whole day in the cool, calm shallows.

The word hippopotamus means river horse. Long ago, people thought hippos were related to horses. A hippo grazes on grass like a horse, lives in a herd like a horse, is as tall as a horse, and makes a sound that is very close to the neighing of a horse.

Following the rules

A young male hippo is uncomfortable and moves. An adult turns to face him, and opens its gigantic mouth. The young one sees the error of his ways. Changing position like that is out of the question!

In one area, the mothers and the babies stay together in a herd led by a large female. The males settle all around them. Each male has fought for his position. The strongest are closest to the females and the weakest are farthest away.

A female hippo is called a cow, a young hippo is a calf, and an adult male is called a bull. The biggest, strongest bull can weigh more than 6,000 pounds!

One big bull watches a dozen cows and calves. He must constantly defend his position against the other bulls.

This one is making a funny face! When a hippo tucks in his lips like this, he is showing respect or apologizing to another hippo for breaking a rule.

What a yawn! Hippos have bigger mouths than any other land mammal!

Hippos come out of the water to mark their territory with their dung.

Terrible teeth

It is midafternoon. One by one, the hippos yawn. The bulls spread their jaws the widest. Hippos yawn when they are tired, but bulls also yawn to show off their teeth! This bull can open his jaws to an angle of more than 150 degrees. The size of a hippo's yawn is a sign of its position and power.

A hippo's canine teeth grow all its life. As sharp as razors, they are dangerous weapons. A hippo can bite a big crocodile right in half! The canine teeth are called tusks, but unlike the tusks of an elephant, which grow from the upper jaw, the tusks of a hippo grow from its lower jaw.

In the heat of the day, the herd of hippos dozes.

The hippo has tiny hairs all over its body and short bristles around its mouth and at the end of its tail.

8

The tusks may grow as long as one of your arms (about 24 inches).

Suddenly, a group of hippos is frightened. They shut their ears and nostrils and dive under water. After several minutes, they come up to the surface again, blowing through their nostrils and wiggling their ears to shake out the water.

Hippos are pretty good swimmers but they prefer to float or move along by walking on the river bed. They like shallow, calm water where they will not be carried along by the current.

When it comes up from underwater, the hippo blows out through its nostrils.

Battle of the bulls

Suddenly, two huge bulls face each other. Snorting water, they hurl themselves toward each other, roaring. Each one threatens to slash with his tusks, making deep cuts on the other. Fortunately, hippos have a thick layer of fat which gives them some protection. This time, however, the bellowing, grunting, and roaring convince the weaker bull to back off without a fight.

The bulls fight often to show their strength and determine their position in the herd. Their wounds have a remarkable ability to heal without becoming infected, in spite of the filthy water.

It is amazing that
these heavy beasts can
climb such steep hills
without slipping!

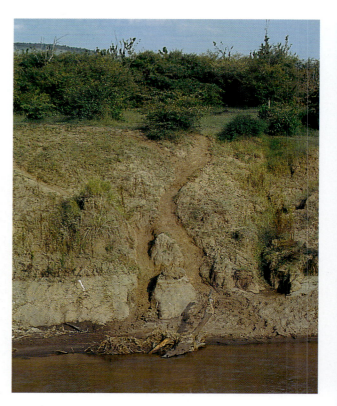

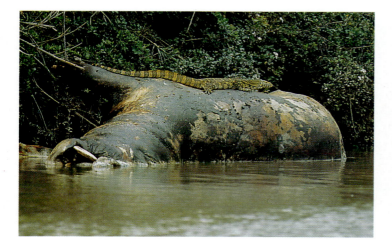

This lizard sits on the
body of a hippo that
died of battle wounds.

For most of the day,
hippos rest. They
sometimes lick their
own skin to lap up the
mineral salts on it.

With its thick legs, huge shovel-shaped head, and big-barrel body, the hippo is a strange looking beast.

The living lawnmower

At nightfall, the hippos leave the water one after the other. They follow well-worn paths to the feeding areas. They like to graze within a few miles of the water where they live. It is now the end of the dry season. The hippos have to go much farther each night to find the 80 to 100 pounds of grass each one eats.

For about 5 hours a night, a hippo uses its lips to break off grass close to the ground. This type of grazing trims the grass as if it had been cut by a lawnmower. The bulls do not fight when they are out of the water. They leave piles of dung, as road signs to help them find their way back.

Hippo, hippo, hooray!

Back in the water as the sun rises, the hippos splash each other and seek out the cool mud to wallow in. They are welcome neighbors to other animals because hippo dung is good fertilizer. The fertilizer makes algae and plants grow in and near the water. Some of these plants are food for a whole bunch of little water creatures that are then eaten by fish. The fishing birds fly quickly to the hippo pool. It's a real feast!

Fish eagle, kingfisher, stork: these and other birds take advantage of the water plants and fish that thrive around hippos.

Hippos have four toes on each foot. The toes are webbed together by thick skin. Each toe has a hoof-like toenail.

The young males crowd together in a mud wallow.

Pink hippo

The rains have finally come. Hippos come out of the water during the cooler days. If they get too warm, they sweat a pinkish oil from special glands in their skin. The pink oil is a natural sunblock that screens out the burning ultraviolet rays. Even so, hippos like to be in the water often, or to cover themselves with mud.

On land hippos can be very dangerous. Don't get between a hippo and the water. A startled hippo can run eight miles an hour, which is much faster than a person. To get back into the water, a frightened hippo will trample anything in its way.

Mud protects a hippo's skin: it gets rid of biting insects such as horseflies and tse-tse flies.

Water babies

It is the rainy season. Eight months have passed since the hippos mated. The baby is born in the water. It can drink its mother's milk on land or underwater. While drinking, the baby hippo can hold its breath for almost two minutes!

Babies are usually born in the water and learn to swim before they learn to walk. Some baby hippos are born on the land.

Crocodiles can catch a baby by surprise. The mother hippo must keep a careful watch over her baby.

Despite the mother's watchfulness, crocodiles in the water, and lions, hyenas, and other predators on land, put the baby hippo in danger everywhere. Almost half the babies die in the first year.

The baby weighs between 60 and 100 pounds at birth and at least 500 pounds after a year!

During the baby's first weeks of life, the mother doesn't leave it, even to eat. She stays close, watching her baby, ready to attack any creature who gets too close on land or in the water. The crocodiles are hungry! The big male hippos nearby might kill the baby so that the female will be ready to mate with one of them.

Young males play at fighting.

One mother babysits for all the young hippos while their mothers eat. Each mother takes a turn being babysitter.

When hippos swim, four webbed toes on each foot help them do the dog paddle.

Bringing up baby

The baby is already a month old. It is ready to join the herd of mothers and babies. The herd stays far away from the bulls, who are dangerous. The older babies are there, too. The big brother is 2 years old, and his older sister is 4 years old.

Baby hippos are very funny. They happily climb onto the back or the neck of their mother and tumble over with their legs up in the air. They play and learn by watching the older hippos.

Around the age of 6 months, a baby may begin to go with its mother at night to eat grass. A young hippo stays with its mother for at least two years, or until she gives birth again.

Growing and changing

After several years, the young male hippo leaves the herd. A hippo is not full grown until the age of ten. Soon he will have to fight for a territory and a mate.

Now life on his own is tough. He can find only a little mud hole, where he hardly has room to turn over and moisten his back. He cannot come near any of the females until he is big enough to fight with the big bulls.

Neighing and yawning and wallowing in the mud, the hippo will never win a beauty contest, but the "river horse" fills a unique position in the African landscape.

Hippo yawns do not scare the long-legged jacana who hunts for creatures that live amid the muck on the hippo's skin.

Fewer and fewer

The hippopotamus is a tough creature and can live for a very long time. It has few enemies when it is grown up. But, even so, there are fewer and fewer hippos every year. Why is that?

For one thing, hippos have a hard time when rivers and lakes dry up. Farmers and fishermen compete with hippos for the water, and poachers shoot hippos for meat and to sell their ivory tusks.

In eastern Zaire, there are over 23,000 hippopotamus herds.

They need a lot of water!

Hippos must have fresh water all year long – not just to drink, but to soak in up to their necks. However, in many parts of Africa, it rains less and less each year, and the rivers dry out for part of the year. The hippos are losing their places to live.

Problems with people

More and more people need land to farm. Land near rivers and lakes, where hippos live, is the most fertile and the easiest to irrigate. Farmers settle there and complain that the hippos eat their crops at night. Fishermen complain, too, about the hippos destroying their nets.

Fishing is dangerous if an angry hippo is nearby.

Sharing the habitat

Hippos don't disturb other animals. In fact, they help some by leaving low grass for buffalo, wart hogs, and other grazers. Unfortunately, when hippos become too crowded, as they did in Uganda and Zaire, they destroy plants by trampling them.

Killed for their tusks

Hippos have been hunted since the Stone Age for their skin, meat, and ivory tusks. Hippo ivory is softer than elephant ivory, so it is easier to carve. Since 1990, when the sale of elephant tusks was stopped, poachers kill more and more hippos for their ivory.

A hippo's tusks are covered by a yellowish enamel. Poachers remove the enamel to uncover the ivory. The ivory ends up weighing a lot less than the original tusk.

Fascinating animals!

Zoologists are currently studying hippopotamus behavior. They have discovered that these great mammals communicate, like whales and elephants, by infrasound – very low sounds that a human can't hear. When a group upstream emits one of these low sounds, another group miles away responds within seconds. Scientists have discovered 7 different calls that can be combined in many ways. When diving, hippos use sound waves to find their way because lake and river waters are often muddy. There is still much to learn about these strange animals.

Some hippos live well near people, as they do here in the fishing town of Vitshumbi in Zaire.

25

Family album

The hippo's only close relative is the pygmy hippopotamus of western Africa. Its next closest relatives are pigs! Scientists put them in the same category because both pigs and hippos have an even number of toes, do not chew their cud, and have tusks. Rhinos may look a lot like hippos, but they don't belong to the same family.

▲

The pygmy hippo weighs no more than 500 pounds, and although it is a good swimmer, it does not spend its days in the water. This little hippo hides alone in the forest, coming out only at night. It is hard to find so no one knows exactly how many there are. With loss of habitat, this endangered animal faces extinction.

◄ The wild boar is closely related to the barnyard pig. This rough-looking character may weigh 350 pounds or more. Instead of using its two-toed feet, it relies on its broad snout to dig in the ground for roots and tubers. Although its eyes are weak, it has a good sense of smell, which helps it find small animals, grains, and leaves to eat. Groups of females and young boars live together in the underbrush of forested areas in Europe, Asia, and North Africa. It was introduced into southern United States forests in 1912 for sport hunting.

▲
When this wart hog baby grows up, its huge face will have several big lumps called warts. Wart hogs live in open plains, or savannas, in family groups. They eat grains and wallow in the mud. They have some very unusual habits. Sometimes they kneel down to eat, with front legs bent. And at the least sign of danger, the wart hogs split up and run in different directions, their tails sticking straight up in the air!